Flynn's Fantastic Flight

Written by
A H Benjamin

Illustrated by
Marcus Gray

Chapter One

Flynn loved bubble gum.

He always had a piece of gum, chewing pink circles in his mouth, round and round.

Flynn loved to blow bubbles. Huge, round, pink spheres.

Flynn's Fantastic Flight

Level 9 – Gold

Helpful Hints for Reading at Home

The focus phonemes (units of sound) used throughout this series are in line with the order in which your child is taught at school. This offers a consistent approach to learning whether reading at home or in the classroom.

HERE ARE SOME COMMON WORDS THAT YOUR CHILD MIGHT FIND TRICKY:

water	where	would	know	thought	through	couldn't
laughed	eyes	once	we're	school	can't	our

TOP TIPS FOR HELPING YOUR CHILD TO READ:

- Encourage your child to read aloud as well as silently to themselves.
- Allow your child time to absorb the text and make comments.
- Ask simple questions about the text to assess understanding.
- Encourage your child to clarify the meaning of new vocabulary.

This book focuses on developing independence, fluency and comprehension. It is a gold level 9 book band.

Bigger and rounder he blew.

Twenty... Thirty... More and more bubbles.

"That's amazing!" said all his friends.

One day, Flynn entered a bubble-blowing show. He won first place! The prize was thirty thousand bubble gum swirls.

They were sent to his house that day.

"These will last me until my birthday!" cried Flynn, excitedly.

At school, Flynn's pockets were bursting with bubble gum swirls. He shared them out.

"I'll blow a bubble so fat and round, it will lift me off the ground!" Flynn boasted.

Flynn threw even more bubble gum swirls into his mouth.

Chomp! Chomp! Chomp!

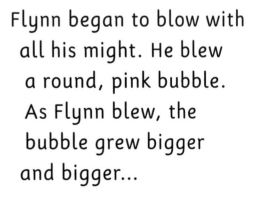

Flynn began to blow with all his might. He blew a round, pink bubble. As Flynn blew, the bubble grew bigger and bigger...

Everybody stared. Their eyes grew wider.
Slowly, Flynn's feet lifted off the ground.

He began to float upwards. Up and up towards
the clouds...

Before anybody could do anything about it,
Flynn and the giant bubble were drifting up,
into the sky!

Chapter Two

Flynn twirled and whirled in the wind.

He looked down. On the ground, his friends were tiny. His teacher, shouting up at him, was no bigger than a mouse.

At first he was scared, but soon he became used to the feeling of flying.

"This is cool!" he thought, excitedly. He could see for miles around.

Flynn drifted like a big, pink cloud, out of the town and over the trees. There was hardly a sound.

Suddenly, a big, black bird flew out of the clouds towards him.

The bird circled around the bubble.

"Oh, no!" Flynn thought. "If it bursts my bubble, I'll fall to the ground!"

He couldn't shout with the bubble in his mouth! How could he scare the bird away?

Flynn had to do something. He put his hands in his pockets and found some things to throw at the bird.

A bubble gum swirl...
A pound coin...
A shiny, brown conker...

But the stubborn bird wouldn't go away. It was flying closer and closer to Flynn's bubble.

Reaching deeper into his pockets, Flynn found his lucky silver marble.

Every time he had played with this marble, he'd won the game.

When it saw the marble, the bird forgot all about the bubble. It was chirping at Flynn, making a loud, screeching sound.

Flynn knew that some birds liked to collect shiny things. He looked at the marble. It was shiny and round. He had never wanted to give it away, but he had to stop that bird.

He held out his hand, hoping to lure the bird with the shiny toy.

The bird swooped down and scooped the marble into its beak. It flew off, swirling down towards its nest in the trees below.

"Phew!" thought Flynn. The bubble was safe.

Chapter Three

Flynn had not gone far when he saw a majestic, red dragon swooping above him.

The dragon seemed to be attached to a string. It was sweeping round and round, through the clouds and down to the ground. Phew! It wasn't a real dragon, with its flaming red eyes and tail lashing about.

It was a kite!

Without warning, the dragon kite whirled towards the bubble.

Whoosh!

It only just missed, then up it went again, spiralling around. It twirled around the bubble again, and then a third time.

Flynn tried to catch the dragon and grab its long tail as it whirled past. But he kept missing.

"This must be how a cat feels trying to pounce on a mouse!" Flynn thought. "I'm all puffed out!"

He needed something he could bash the kite with as it swirled around him. But there were no weapons to be seen!

With a bit of a struggle, Flynn reached down and took off one of his shoes.

He held the laces firmly in his hand and swung the shoe round in a circle.

"This should do the trick," Flynn thought. He was proud of his brainwave.

Just then, the dragon swirled towards him once more.

Flynn knew he had to hit it with his first try. He must not hit the bubble! Aiming carefully, he began to swing his shoe faster. It made a whooshing sound.

He let go – just as the kite came closer to him. The shoe shot through the air and then...

CRASH!

It struck the dragon, which fell through the clouds towards the ground, with the shoe following close behind it.

"Whoopeee!" Flynn felt like shrieking.

Chapter Four

Flynn was soaring over the countryside. Everything looked small and far away.

Beneath him he could see the leafy tops of the silver birch trees around the park. A circus was arriving. Their wagons, painted all different colours, looked like toys.

It all looked so strange that Flynn hardly noticed until it was too late.

A huge group of hot air balloons had appeared all around him! There were at least thirty giant, round balloons! He was surrounded.

"What shall I do?" Flynn thought. "I do not want to get stuck to a balloon!"

The balloons were everywhere.

Flynn's feet hit a balloon. Without thinking, he crouched and pushed... And bounced off and away!

That was fun! Flynn bounced and jumped from balloon to balloon. Up, up, UP!

He bounced up and down and all around until his head was dizzy.

He was almost clear of the balloons!

Suddenly, Flynn's shoelace caught on the skirt of the biggest balloon. It had wound around the ropes and was dragging Flynn with it!

"Ouch!" thought Flynn. "My foot!"

He didn't want to be dragged away.

Flynn spun twice in the air. He wobbled and whirled, and the sky was spinning before his eyes.

He squirmed about and managed to kick his shoe with his other foot until it fell off. He was free!

Flynn floated upwards towards the clouds.

"That was close," Flynn thought, closing his mouth firmly around the gum. "And I've lost both shoes now."

He wondered what his mum would say.

Chapter Five

Flynn thought he might like to get back to the ground soon.

He was wondering how, when he spotted three dots in the distance. They grew bigger and bigger as they approached.

"Now what?" Flynn wondered, nervously.

He soon found out. A team of three jet fighters flew towards him, with streams of red, blue and orange smoke trailing behind them. They must be practising for an air show.

"I need to get out of here!" thought Flynn, as the bubble spun again.

The jets roared past Flynn. Both he and the bubble twisted in the air.

He wanted to yell "Look out!" but the bubble would have fallen out of his mouth.

The noise died away and the planes vanished in a great cloud of swirling colours.

Flynn was glad he was still in one piece. But what about the bubble?

The bubble was dirty with red, blue and orange smoke. And... was that a little hole there? With air leaking out?

Sure enough, the bubble was losing air. Slowly, Flynn started to sink towards the ground.

Chapter Six

Before long, Flynn was flying low over the outskirts of the town.

People began to notice him. They stared and pointed. Some hollered up at him.

"Is it a bird?" they cried. Flynn skimmed over treetops and weaved between the roofs of houses. He knocked a chimney pot with his bare foot.

"Ouch!" he almost shouted, nearly forgetting about the gum. He bit down firmly.

"I will never blow a bubble as big as this again," Flynn promised himself.

He looked all around. He could see his house!
The first one on the street.

Flynn's mum was hanging the washing out. He
landed softly next to the birdbath.

"Hi, Mum," said Flynn chirpily.

The bubble ran out of air at last. It drooped down over Flynn, covering him from head to toe. He looked like a creature from another planet.

Startled, Flynn's mum spun around. She screamed, then rushed into the house.

"Oh dear," sighed Flynn. "I guess I have a lot of explaining to do!"

Flynn's Fantastic Flight

1. How many bubble gum swirls did Flynn win?

2. What do you think Flynn's teacher was shouting up at him?

3. What did Flynn hit the dragon kite with?

4. What did Flynn's shoelace get caught on?
   (a) The skirt of the balloon
   (b) The dragon kite string
   (c) The washing line

5. How do you think Flynn felt when he was floating in the sky? Can you think of a time that you've felt like this?

©This edition published 2021.
First published in 2020.
BookLife Publishing Ltd.
King's Lynn, Norfolk PE30 4LS

ISBN 978-1-83927-011-6

Flynn's Fantastic Flight
Written by A H Benjamin
Illustrated by Marcus Gray

An Introduction to BookLife Readers...

Our Readers have been specifically created in line with the London Institute of Education's approach to book banding and are phonetically decodable and ordered to support each phase of the Letters and Sounds document.

Each book has been created to provide the best possible reading and learning experience. Our aim is to share our love of books with children, providing both emerging readers and prolific page-turners with beautiful books that are guaranteed to provoke interest and learning, regardless of ability.

BOOK BAND GRADED using the Institute of Education's approach to levelling.

PHONETICALLY DECODABLE supporting each phase of Letters and Sounds.

EXERCISES AND QUESTIONS to offer reinforcement and to ascertain comprehension.

BEAUTIFULLY ILLUSTRATED to inspire and provoke engagement, providing a variety of styles for the reader to enjoy whilst reading through the series.

This book focuses on developing independence, fluency and comprehension. It is a gold level 9 book band.

For Flynn.